SHINO AND THE CHAOS CREW

The Day the RAIN FELL UP

Written by Chris Callaghan

Illustrated by Amit Tayal

Collins

Shinoy and the Chaos Crew

When Shinoy downloads the Chaos Crew app on his phone, a glitch in the system gives him the power to summon his TV heroes into his world.

With the team on board, Shinoy can figure out what dastardly plans the red-eyed S.N.A.I.R., a Super Nasty Artificial Intelligent Robot, has come up with, and save the day.

When Shinoy opened his bedroom curtains, he could see that something wasn't quite right. It had been raining for days but today it didn't look *normal*.

The rain wasn't falling down from the sky; it was falling up from the ground!

When strange things happened, there was only one thing to do.

Shinoy activated the special app on his phone. "Call to Action, Chaos Crew!"

Shinoy's phone buzzed. A burst of light shot out as Ember from the Chaos Crew appeared, ready for action.

"Where's the fire?" asked Ember.

Shinoy grinned. "Actually, it's the exact opposite – water!"

They ran out into the front garden.
Shinoy's best friend, Toby, was already there.

"Hey, Shinoy. Hi, Ember. The rain's going up
my pyjamas!" he laughed.

Shinoy sneezed. "It's gone up my nose!"

Ember didn't look happy. "I don't like rain
when it's normal, but this is weird!"

"What's going on?" shouted Dad from the doorway.

"The rain's falling up," Shinoy shouted back.

"That can't be good for the garden."

"It's not good for anything," said Ember, pointing to the neighbour's pond. "I need to see what's happening in the sky."

Ember unclipped her backpack. She was
the last of the Phoenix People and inside
the bag were her wings. She unfolded
them gently.

"I'm coming with you," said Shinoy.
He wasn't going to miss a chance to fly!

Ember clipped on a harness and
Shinoy was lifted off the ground.

"Make sure you're
back for breakfast,"
called Mum.
"You have PE
first lesson!"

Shinoy waved at Mum.

"I probably should've changed
out of my pyjamas," he said.

"No time!" said Ember. "Look!"

8

Huge fountains of water were shooting into the sky from the river. It was almost dry.

"The same thing will be happening to the drinking water," Shinoy puffed.

It was damp and cold inside the clouds and Shinoy began shaking.

Ember laughed. "You don't have central heating like me."

Ember glowed and Shinoy felt warmth filling him like a mug of hot chocolate.

"I can feel cold streams
within the clouds,"
said Ember. "I'm going to see
where they lead to. Hold on!"

Ember's enormous wings flapped as they followed the mysterious cold streams. The water was being pulled away from the ground by some kind of giant fluffy magnet.

Bursting out of the clouds, Ember and Shinoy found themselves heading straight towards a factory.

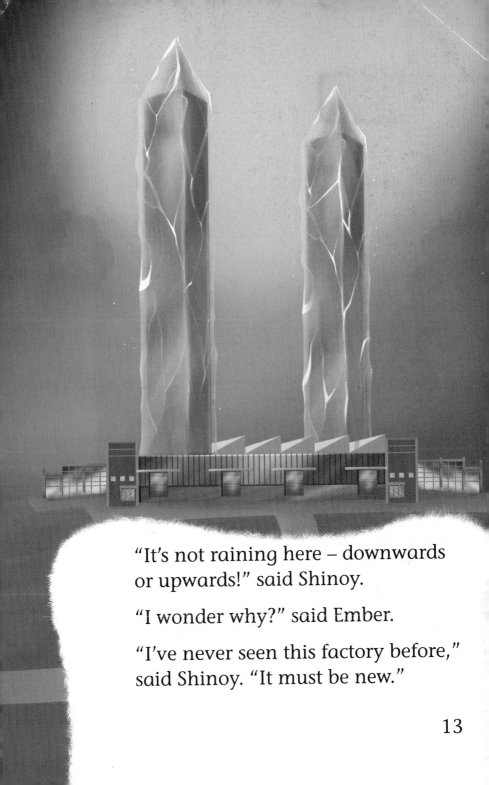

"It's not raining here – downwards or upwards!" said Shinoy.

"I wonder why?" said Ember.

"I've never seen this factory before," said Shinoy. "It must be new."

13

As they
flew nearer,
Ember said,
"The coldness
is coming from
those towers."

14

They landed outside the factory and Ember put her wings back in her backpack.

The sign on the building read: Cooler than Cool Ice Cube Company.

"Oi!" shouted a man, running out of the factory. "This is private property. And you shouldn't just be wearing pyjamas, young man, it's too cold for that. I'm an expert on cold, you know."

"The cold from your towers is messing with the weather," said Ember.

"The super-cold air is how we make the coldest and coolest ice cubes in the world. *Cooler than cool,*" the man said proudly.

16

"Your factory is making it rain upside down. The water is being sucked away from the town," Shinoy shouted.

"You're obviously sleepwalking," the man laughed. Shinoy was sure his eyes flashed red, like the evil S.N.A.I.R.'s! The man ran back into the factory and slammed the door with a *BANG*.

Ember spread her wings once more. "We can fix this."

17

Shinoy and Ember
circled the factory.

"Metal will melt if it's
hot enough," Shinoy
said. "I'm sure I know
someone who can do that."

Ember released a blast of fire towards the towers. The heat made Shinoy's face feel hotter than a double-chilli pizza straight out of the oven. He could feel the power from Ember as the fire melted the metal and sealed the extra-cold air inside the towers.

19

They flew away from the factory, but water was still shooting upwards.

"It's as cold as the Forbidden Wasteland," said Ember.

"That was my favourite episode in series 4!" said Shinoy. "You warmed me up before – can't you do the same for the sky?"

Ember glowed.

As they arrived back in Shinoy's garden, there was a RUMBLE.

Ember grinned. "Where there's thunder, there's lightning and –"

"Rain!" Shinoy cheered, as rain fell *down* from the sky.

"I thought you'd need cooling down after your trip," Mum smiled, "so I've put some ice in your orange juice!"

Chaos Crew weather report

rainy

stormy

fishy

frosty

hot

very hot

cloudy

warm

icy

rainy

fishy

ice-cool

Ideas for reading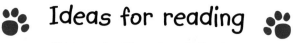

Written by Clare Dowdall, PhD
Lecturer and Primary Literacy Consultant

Reading objectives

- discuss the sequence of events in books and how items of information are related
- make inferences on the basis of what is being said and done
- predict what might happen on the basis of what has been read so far
- explain and discuss their understanding of books, poems and other material, both those that they listen to and those that they read for themselves.

Spoken language objectives

- participate in discussions, presentations, performances and debates
- gain, maintain and monitor the interest of the listener(s)

Curriculum links: Science – working scientifically; Geography – physical geography: the water cycle

Word count: 835

Interest words: Ember, phoenix, harness, central heating.

Resources: ice cube trays, different liquids for freezing, access to a freezer, ICT for research, pens and pencils.

Build a context for reading

- Look at the front cover and read the title *The Day the Rain Fell Up*. Ask children what is strange about this title.
- Ask children to explain what they know about the rain: where does it come from; why does it fall downwards; what happens to the rain if it is warm or cold when it rains?
- Challenge children to suggest why the rain is falling up in the story and what might be causing this to happen.

Understand and apply reading strategies

- Read pp2–3. Ask children what they would do and how they would feel if they saw rain falling up from the ground? Would they be worried?

In the best books, the ending often comes as a shock.
Not just because of that one last twist in the tale,
but because you have been so absorbed in their world,
that coming back to the harsh light of reality is a jolt.

If that describes you now, then perhaps you should track down
some new leads, and find new suspense in other worlds.

Join us at www.hodder.co.uk, or follow us on
Twitter @hodderbooks, and you can tap in to a
community of fellow thrill-seekers.

Whether you want to find out more about this book,
or a particular author, watch trailers and interviews, have
the chance to win early limited editions, or simply browse
our expert readers' selection of the very best books,
we think you'll find what you're looking for.

And if you don't, that's the place to tell us what's missing.

We love what we do, and we'd love you to be part of it.

www.hodder.co.uk

@hodderbooks

HodderBooks

HodderBooks